D0949983

MAGIC TREE HOUSE®

#32 To the Future, Ben Franklin!

Dear Reader,

Did you know there's a Magic Tree House® book for every kid? From those just starting to read chapter books to more experienced readers, Magic Tree House® has something for everyone, including science, sports, geography, wildlife, history . . . and always a bit of mystery and magic!

Magic Tree House®
Adventures with Jack and Annie, perfect for readers who are just starting to read chapter books.
F&P Level: M

Magic Tree House®
Merlin Missions
More challenging adventures for the experienced Magic Tree House® reader.
F&P Levels: M–N

Magic Tree House®
Super Edition
A longer and more dangerous adventure with Jack and Annie.
F&P Level: P

Magic Tree House®
Fact Trackers
Nonfiction companions to your favorite Magic Tree House® adventures.
F&P Levels: N–X

Happy reading!

MAGIC TREE HOUSE®

#32 To the Future, Ben Franklin!

BY MARY POPE OSBORNE

ILLUSTRATED BY AG FORD

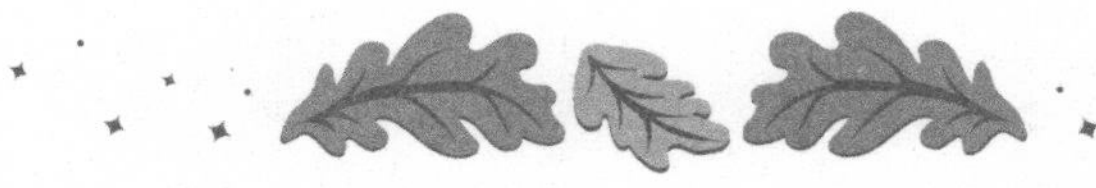

A STEPPING STONE BOOK™

Random House New York

This is a work of fiction. All incidents and dialogue, and all characters with the exception of some well-known historical and public figures, are products of the author's imagination and are not to be construed as real. Where real-life historical or public figures appear, the situations, incidents, and dialogues concerning those persons are fictional and are not intended to depict actual events or to change the fictional nature of the work. In all other respects, any resemblance to persons living or dead is entirely coincidental.

 Published in the United States by Random House Children's Books, a division of Penguin Random House LLC, New York.

Random House and the colophon are registered trademarks and A Stepping Stone Book and the colophon are trademarks of Penguin Random House LLC.

Magic Tree House is a registered trademark of Mary Pope Osborne; used under license.

Visit us on the Web!
rhcbooks.com
MagicTreeHouse.com

Educators and librarians, for a variety of teaching tools, visit us at
RHTeachersLibrarians.com

Library of Congress Cataloging-in-Publication Data is available upon request.
ISBN 978-0-525-64832-1 (trade) — ISBN 978-0-525-64833-8 (lib. bdg.) —
ISBN 978-0-525-64834-5 (ebook)

Printed in the United States of America
10 9 8 7 6 5 4 3 2 1

This book has been officially leveled by using the F&P Text Level Gradient™ Leveling System.

Random House Children's Books supports the First Amendment and celebrates the right to read.

For the Harne Family

George

Debbie

Sophia

Elliot

Beatrice

Abigail

Lillian

CONTENTS

PROLOGUE

One summer day in Frog Creek, Pennsylvania, a mysterious tree house appeared in the woods. It was filled with books. A boy named Jack and his sister, Annie, found the tree house and soon discovered that it was magic. They could go to any time and place in history just by pointing to a picture in one of the books. While they were gone, no time at all passed back in Frog Creek.

Jack and Annie eventually found out that the tree house belonged to Morgan le Fay, a magical librarian from the legendary realm of Camelot.

Since then, they have traveled on many adventures in the magic tree house and completed many missions for Morgan.

On their journeys to New York, Texas, and the Roman Empire, Jack and Annie learned great wisdom from three heroes of the past. Now they're about to journey back in time to learn from a fourth hero!

1

NO JOKE

It was a hot summer afternoon.

Jack and Annie sat in their living room. Jack was reading a book about weather. Annie was looking out the window.

"Let's go do something," she said.

"Too hot," said Jack.

"We could ride our bikes to the lake," Annie said. "And go swimming."

"No way," said Jack.

"We could—"

"Shh, please," said Jack. "I'm trying to read."

Annie was quiet for a moment. Then she gasped.

"Oh, wow, lightning! I just saw a flash of lightning out there," she said.

"You're joking," said Jack. "Nice try."

"No joke! I saw it!" said Annie.

"There's not a single cloud," said Jack. "You need clouds to have lightning."

"Then it must have been . . . *magic*!" said Annie. "Come on, let's go!"

"No, thanks. Have fun," said Jack.

"You'll be sorry," said Annie as she rushed outside.

Jack waited for Annie to come back in from the heat. He waited and waited. But she didn't return.

Jack put down his book. "I'd better check," he said to himself. He picked up his backpack and headed outside.

Oh, man, Jack thought as he headed up the sidewalk. *It must be a hundred degrees in the sun.*

By the time Jack reached the Frog Creek woods, he was sweaty and out of breath. He crossed the street and walked between the trees. Even in the shade, the air was muggy.

Jack tramped through the woods until he came to the tallest oak.

"Hey there," said Annie. She was leaning against the trunk of the tree. *Next to a dangling rope ladder.*

"I told you it was no joke," said Annie.

"Right. No joke," Jack said with a grin.

Annie grabbed the ladder and started up.

Jack followed. As they climbed into the magic tree house, golden sunlight slanted across the floor. The warm wood had a deep, rich smell of summer. In a shadowy corner was a piece of parchment.

"A note from Morgan," said Jack. He picked up the note and read aloud:

In Old Philadelphia,
A paper must be signed.
Help Doctor Ben
Make up his mind.

"Doctor Ben?" said Jack. "Is Ben his last name or first name?"

Annie shrugged. "I don't know," she said. "Keep reading."

Jack kept reading:

To get his attention,
Say "We're from the press."
Then do what you can
To ease his distress.

Listen to his thoughts.
If his fears start to grow
And he loses all hope,
There's a place he must go.

'Tis a land filled with things
You see every day.
But these everyday wonders
Will show him the way.

"Hmm," said Annie. "So Morgan wants us to go to Old Philadelphia. We have to find someone named Doctor Ben. Then we need to help him make up his mind to sign some kind of paper. That sounds easy."

"Yeah, definitely easier than going to a Roman army camp or an island about to have one of the worst hurricanes in American history," said Jack.

"Philadelphia's not that far from Frog Creek," said Annie. "They're both in Pennsylvania."

"Yep, my class took a field trip there," said Jack. "It's not that far in *miles*. But 'old' could mean we're going far back in time."

"That's okay. '*Old* Philadelphia' sounds charming," said Annie.

"Charming?" said Jack.

"Yeah, like lovely and pleasant," said Annie.

"Okay!" said Jack. "So, where's our research book?"

They looked around. The only book in the tree house was their Pennsylvania book—the book that always brought them back home.

"Hold on," said Jack. "I have an idea." He picked up the Pennsylvania book and checked the table of contents. "Yes! There's a chapter called 'Old Philadelphia, 1787.'"

"Cool, let's go to 1787!" said Annie. "This book can take us there *and* bring us back home."

"Exactly," said Jack. He turned to a page that showed a drawing of a cobblestone street with women in long dresses, and carts pulled by horses.

"See, it *does* look charming!" said Annie. "Let's go!"

"Right," said Jack. He pointed to the drawing. "I wish we could go there!"

The wind started to blow.

The tree house started to spin.

It spun faster and faster.

Then everything was still.

Absolutely still.

2

OLD PHILADELPHIA

The sun was high in the hazy sky. The air was still and muggy.

"Ugh," said Jack. "It's just as hot here as it was at home."

"Yeah, and our clothes are going to make us even hotter," said Annie. She was wearing a long dress with long sleeves, an apron, buckle shoes, and stockings.

Jack was wearing knee-high wool pants, a white shirt with a vest, buckle shoes, and stockings. His backpack was now a leather bag.

"Louis!" a woman called nearby. "Louis!"

Jack and Annie peeked out the window. The tree house had landed in a wide, shady tree in a walled courtyard.

"Louis!" the person called again.

Annie pushed back a branch to see better. Near the tree was a two-story brick house. The woman calling to Louis stood in the doorway. She wore a long dark dress and a white bonnet.

A man digging in the garden looked up.

"He's gone swimming, Miss Sarah," the man said.

"Oh, dear. I've prepared a midday meal for my father," said Miss Sarah. "Louis was supposed to take it to him."

"I could take it, ma'am," said the gardener.

"Oh, thank you, John!" the woman said. "It's on the kitchen table. Please carry it to the old state house and deliver it to Doctor Ben. I have to go out shopping for a while."

"Yes, ma'am," said the gardener. He put down his shovel and headed into the house.

"Doctor Ben!" Annie whispered to Jack. "That's who we're supposed to find! I told you it would be easy."

"Right," said Jack. "But who is he? What does he do?"

"I don't know," said Annie. "But we'll find out if we take his lunch to him! Come on, Jack! We have to act fast!" She started down the rope ladder.

Jack quickly put their Pennsylvania book in his bag. He climbed down the ladder and joined Annie in the courtyard.

"We should hide the ladder and pretend we walked here," said Jack. He lifted the bottom of the rope ladder and tucked it behind a low branch of the tree.

John, the gardener, came out of the house. He was carrying a small covered basket.

"Excuse me!" Annie called to him. "Is Louis here?"

"Everybody's looking for Louis today," the man said. "I'm afraid he's gone swimming."

"Oh, no!" said Annie. "We're friends of his. We're supposed to go with him to the old state house—"

"To take the midday meal to his grandfather," said Jack.

"Louis must have forgotten," said the gardener.

"Well, I guess we could take it without him," said Annie, "if you'd like us to."

"Why, yes," the gardener said. "I still have a lot of work to do." He handed Annie the basket and wiped his brow. "This is the hottest summer in forty years."

"No problem! We can handle it," said Annie. "Come on, Jack!" She started out of the courtyard.

"Hold on!" said Jack. He turned back to the

gardener. "Excuse me, sir. Can you tell me something about Doctor Ben? Who is he? What does he do?"

"What does he *do*?" the gardener said. "It would take me all day to answer that question!"

"Oh. Sorry, we—" said Jack.

But the gardener kept talking. "He's one of the smartest human beings of all time. He once stole thunderbolts right out of the clouds."

"Oh. Okay," said Jack. *Is this guy trying to be funny?* he wondered.

"He's an inventor and a scientist!" John the gardener went on. "A diplomat and a writer! A scholar and a businessman!"

"Excuse me, I have to go now," said Jack.

He looked around for Annie. She had already left the courtyard. He headed down the path to the gate.

"There's no one in the universe like him!" the

gardener called after Jack. "I'm telling you the truth. He pulled lightning right out of the clouds!"

Poor guy's been in the heat too long, Jack thought. He waved goodbye and hurried out of the courtyard. He didn't see Annie anywhere!

Jack ran down a short alley to a dirty, noisy cobblestone street. The street was full of wagons and buggies. There were shops and houses on either side.

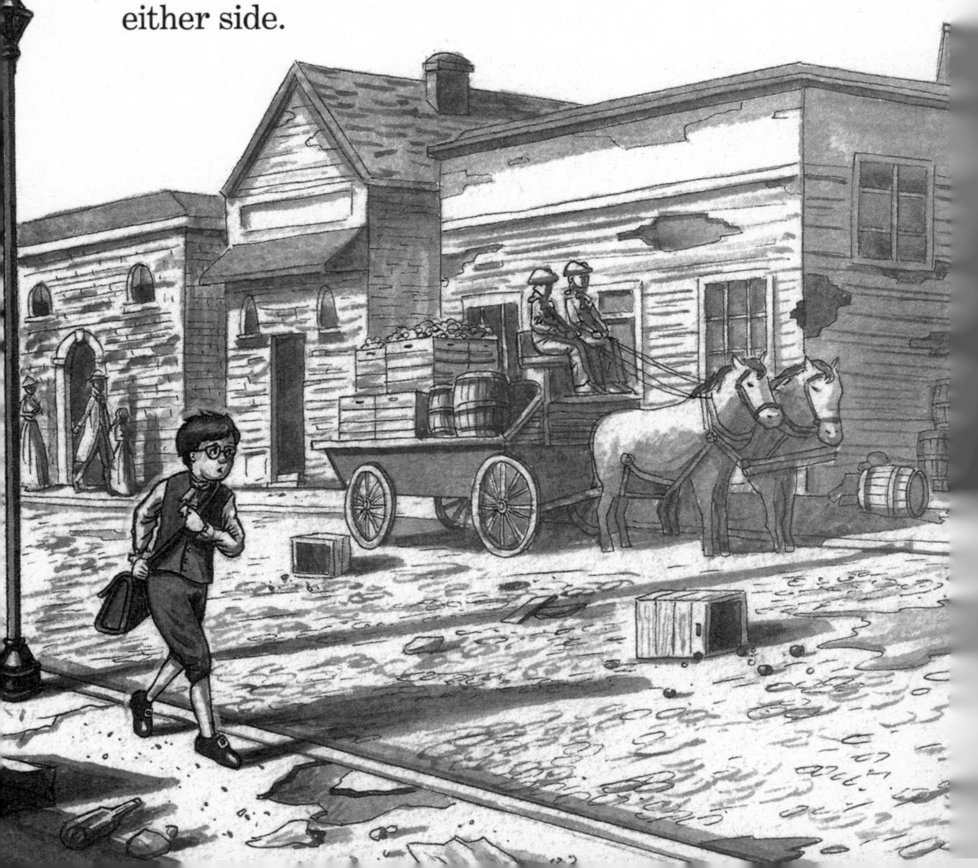

Jack looked around for Annie.

"Jack!" Annie ran to him, carrying the food basket. "Where were you?"

"I tried to ask the gardener about Doctor Ben," said Jack. "But the guy didn't make sense."

"Don't worry. We'll find out soon," said Annie. "I got directions. We go down Market Street, turn left onto Fifth, then right onto Chestnut."

"Let's go," said Jack.

Jack and Annie squeezed past shoppers. They wove around carts loaded with fish and fruit. They stepped over garbage littering the cobblestones. They passed by crowded, smelly horse stables.

"Phew!" said Annie.

"Yeah, bad!" said Jack, holding his nose. With his other hand, he waved at the blue flies buzzing around his head.

No wonder the gardener didn't want to deliver Doctor Ben's food basket! thought Jack. Charming Old Philadelphia didn't seem charming at all!

3

An Important Paper

"Stop," said Annie. "We turn here, onto Fifth Street, then onto Chestnut Street."

Jack and Annie trudged through the heat until they came to Chestnut Street. It was much quieter and calmer than Market.

"Look, that's it," said Jack. He pointed to a brick building with paned windows and a tall bell tower. A sign in front said PENNSYLVANIA STATE HOUSE.

"Great," said Annie. "So this is the plan. We

say we're delivering Doctor Ben's midday meal. Then, to get his attention, we say we're from the press. That's what the rhyme tells us to do."

"Got it," said Jack. "Let's go."

Jack and Annie walked up a pebbled path to the state house. When they reached the brick building, they knocked on the front door. No one came to let them in. Annie tried to turn the door's handle, but it was locked. Looking around, Jack noticed that all the windows were closed. Most of the blinds were drawn.

"No one's here," he said. He felt sweaty and tired from the humid heat. "We came here for nothing."

"Darn," said Annie. "Maybe we should go back to Doctor Ben's house and wait for him there."

Suddenly the door swung open. A guard in a blue jacket and white pants stood before them.

He looks like a soldier from the American Revolution, Jack thought.

"No guests are allowed to enter," the guard said.

"But, sir, we're not guests," Annie said politely. "We're delivering a midday meal to Doctor Ben. It's from his daughter, Miss Sarah."

"All right, come in," said the guard. He moved away from the door.

"Thanks!" said Annie.

She and Jack stepped into the building.

"The doctor is in the Assembly Room," the guard said, pointing down the hall. "Wait outside the room until they take a break."

"Yes, sir," said Jack.

Jack and Annie tiptoed down the dark, shadowy hallway.

"Listen," said Annie. Loud voices were coming from a room ahead. The door was half-open, so she and Jack peeked inside.

"This must be the Assembly Room," whispered Jack.

The large room had high ceilings and two fireplaces. The tall windows were framed by heavy drapes.

Men sat at tables with green tablecloths. They wore long jackets and shirts with white ruffled collars. They all had hair that came to their shoulders.

At the front of the room, a white-haired man sat on a raised platform in a high-backed chair. He seemed to be in charge. Another man stood at a front table, hurriedly writing.

Several men were talking:

"Gentlemen, you are wrong!"

"No! You want to give too much power to the national government."

"He is correct!"

"But we have no Bill of Rights!"

"Or freedom of speech!"

"What about trial by jury?"

The man in charge banged a gavel against his desk. "Order!" he said. "Raise your hands if you wish to speak."

"What's going on?" Annie whispered to Jack.

"I'm not sure," Jack whispered back. "I'll check our book."

He reached into his bag and pulled out their Pennsylvania book. He opened to the chapter about Old Philadelphia. He turned the page.

"Whoa!" Jack whispered. He showed Annie a painting in the book. "Look—it's the same!"

Annie looked at the painting, then back at the men in the room.

"It's *this* meeting!" Annie whispered. "What's going on?"

They read silently:

In 1787, after the Revolutionary War, America was made up of thirteen separate colonies. Each was like a different country. Would the colonies remain separate or become a nation of states? That summer, fifty-five delegates met in Philadelphia to answer this question. James Madison took daily notes on the meetings. In the end, he wrote America's most important document.

Oh, man! thought Jack. He understood everything now.

"Annie—"

"I get it!" she whispered. She repeated a line from Morgan's message: *"A paper must be signed."*

"I know," whispered Jack. "They're creating the *United States Constitution*!"

"The Constitution? That's a big deal," whispered Annie.

"A *huge* deal!" whispered Jack. He and Annie read more:

The document was the United States Constitution. It contained the basic laws that defined how the American government works. The Constitution created the presidency, the Supreme Court, and the Congress.

James Madison's work made him known as the Father of the Constitution. Besides Madison, some of the most famous delegates were General George Washington, Alexander Hamilton, and Dr. Benjamin Franklin.

"Doctor Ben!" said Jack.

"I think I see him!" whispered Annie.

"Where?" said Jack.

"There!" said Annie. "The old man in the glasses."

Annie pointed to an older man with wispy gray hair and glasses. He was wiping his face with a handkerchief.

"Yes!" whispered Jack. "That's Dr. Benjamin Franklin!"

4

"How Strange . . ."

"Benjamin Franklin," Annie whispered.

"I can't believe it," said Jack.

"I've seen him on posters at home," said Annie, "for a show at the Little Theater—*Ben Franklin in Paris.*"

"Right," said Jack. *The gardener was making sense after all,* he thought. Jack knew that Benjamin Franklin was a scientist, an inventor, a diplomat, a writer, and almost everything else you could think of.

"Where's George Washington?" whispered Annie.

"He must be in front," said Jack. He pointed to the white-haired man in the high-backed chair on the platform.

The general was much older than he was when they'd met him in 1776, but he still looked strong and powerful.

"I wonder if he'll remember us," whispered Annie.

"I hope he doesn't," said Jack. "He's a lot older and we're not. That would be hard to explain."

"That man writing must be James Madison," said Annie. She pointed to the small thin man writing at the front table.

George Washington banged his gavel again and rose from his chair.

"We must stop now," he said. "Let us put aside our differences and enjoy a meal together."

The delegates began rising from their chairs. Some were still grumbling and shaking their heads.

George Washington walked over to Ben Franklin. Ben leaned on his walking stick as the two men spoke quietly.

"Let's go," said Annie.

"Wait," said Jack. "We need to plan what to say to him!" But before he could stop her, Annie hurried across the room with Ben's food basket.

Oh, man, thought Jack, following her.

Ben caught sight of them. "Hello, children," he said with a friendly smile.

George Washington looked startled when he saw Jack and Annie. "Have we met before?" he asked in his deep, calm voice.

"Uh . . . actually . . . ," Annie started, but then stopped.

Jack shook his head.

"I know!" said George Washington. "You

remind me of two children I met during the war. How strange . . ."

"Really?" said Annie.

"Yes, they were remarkable!" said George Washington. "But that was eleven years ago—they would be grown by now. I've thought of them often." Jack glanced at Annie, trying to hide a smile.

"What can we do for you, children?" Ben asked.

"Sir, we brought your midday meal. It's from your daughter, Sarah," said Annie. She held out the basket of food.

"Oh, well, thank you," said Ben, chuckling. He set the basket down on the nearest table. "Celery and cabbage, no doubt. Sarah's always trying to keep me healthy."

George Washington smiled. "Enjoy your meal, my friend," he said to Ben. "If you'd prefer steak pie and beer, join us at the tavern." With a nod to Jack and Annie, George Washington left them.

"Tell me, how did you happen to deliver my meal today?" Ben asked Annie. His eyes were bright with curiosity. "I was expecting Louis."

"Um, Louis was supposed to bring it," said Annie. "But he went swimming. So we told John we would do it."

"How kind of you," said Ben. "And what are your names?"

"Jack and Annie," said Jack.

"Well, thank you very much, Jack and Annie," said Ben Franklin. "And good day to both of you."

As Ben started to walk away, Jack remembered Morgan's message. "Sir," he blurted out, "we're from the press."

Ben whirled around. "The press? The *Gazette*?" he whispered.

"Uh . . . yes?" Jack answered. What was the *Gazette*? he wondered.

"No! No! Oh, dear, no!" whispered Ben. "The *Gazette* is sending children to report on us!" He looked around anxiously. "We must leave at once! Come quickly! Follow me!"

Using his walking stick, Ben hobbled to the doorway of the Assembly Room.

Jack was confused. What had they done?

"Sir—sir," he said as they rushed down the hallway after Ben. "We're actually—"

"Quiet! Quiet! Not here! Not another word here! That way! Out the back!" said Ben. Using his cane, he hurried to the back of the state house.

"This way! Come with me!" he said. He opened the door and stepped outside.

Jack and Annie followed Ben Franklin into the burning summer heat.

5

Lightning Rod Ben

Benjamin Franklin leaned against the back door of the state house. His hand trembled as he pulled out his handkerchief.

"Are you all right, sir?" Annie asked.

"Fine . . . I'm fine," said Ben, wiping his face. "But I cannot be seen with you. It would be a disaster. We must move away from here."

Jack and Annie started walking with Ben toward the front of the building.

"But, sir, why would it be a disaster?" asked Annie.

"All the delegates have sworn an oath of secrecy!" said Ben. "I'm sorry to say they've already caught me saying a few things outside of our meetings."

"An oath of secrecy?" said Jack.

"Yes! We believe in freedom of the press," said Ben. "But we need to make a plan first. Not a word of our plan should be printed in the *Gazette*—not until we agree on a plan. . . . Oh, dear . . ."

"The *Gazette*?" said Jack.

"Yes! The *Pennsylvania Gazette.* The very paper I once owned!" said Ben.

"Oh . . . oh, wait," said Annie. "We don't work for the *Pennsylvania Gazette.*"

"No?" said Ben. "But you said you were from the press."

"I know. But we were talking about the *Frog Creek News,*" Annie said. "It's our own little paper. Mine and Jack's. We're the only ones who—who read it."

"She's right," Jack said. "It's just a game we play. We *pretend* to be reporters from the *Frog Creek News* whenever we meet new people."

Ben Franklin stopped walking. He looked hard at Jack and Annie. His expression changed from worry to relief. Then he laughed. "I believe you!" he said. "My goodness, your little game nearly gave me a heart attack!"

"I'm sorry," said Annie.

At least we got his attention, thought Jack.

"So, where do you live?" Ben asked.

"Frog Creek," said Jack. "It's miles away."

"We're tourists," said Annie. "Our parents want us to study history."

"*Tourists?* I'm afraid I do not know that word," said Ben.

"Oh. Well, you can also think of us as 'visiting scholars,'" said Jack. Emperor Marcus Aurelius of Rome had called them "visiting scholars" on their last adventure. Jack liked the sound of that.

Ben seemed to like it, too. His face brightened.

"Ah! Visiting scholars! And so young! That's delightful!" he said. "Come, let us walk, scholars! I'll show you Philadelphia's free library."

Ben started up Chestnut Street. He still used his walking stick. But now he had a little skip in his step.

People waved cheerfully at Ben from wagons and carriages, and he waved back. He seemed to know everyone.

"It's important for visiting scholars to see the very first public library in the colonies," Ben told Jack and Annie. "But I do apologize for the heat."

"Don't worry. You didn't cause it," said Annie.

Ben laughed. "I like your wit, my dear," he said.

"I like yours, too," said Annie.

Ben stopped and pointed his walking stick at a brick building with high, arched windows. "That's it! Our library! I was the founder! Library members—and visiting scholars—can borrow books anytime."

"That's great," said Jack.

"It looks a lot like our Frog Creek Public—" Annie began. But Jack stopped her with a quick shake of his head. He knew there were hardly any public libraries in 1787.

"Hey, Lightning Rod Ben!" a boy shouted from a passing wagon. "Hot enough for you?"

Ben waved at the boy.

"Why did he call you that?" said Annie.

"I invented lightning rods!" said Ben. "I'm surprised you didn't know that. See, there's one." He pointed to a long metal rod that rose up from the roof of the library.

"The lightning hits the rod and then passes through a wire into the earth, right?" said Jack.

"Exactly!" said Ben.

"It keeps the lightning from passing into the building and causing a fire," said Annie.

"My word, you are both *very* bright!" said Ben. He seemed happy and relaxed now. "As visiting scholars, what would you most like to learn about on your visit?"

"You!" Annie and Jack said together.

"Oh, my." Ben chuckled. "Well, perhaps I could tell you a bit about myself while we sit in the courtyard of my house. How does that sound?"

"Cool," said Jack.

"Cool indeed!" said Ben. "We will be much cooler under the shade of my mulberry tree!"

6

Under the Mulberry Tree

Ben led Jack and Annie down Market Street. Pigs and chickens crossed their path. Horse-drawn carts clattered over the dirty cobblestones. But the heat and smells didn't seem so bad now.

"We're here! Come along!" said Ben.

Jack and Annie followed Ben down the alley to his courtyard.

"Please, sit!" said Ben. He motioned to chairs under the shade of the mulberry tree—*the same tree that hid the magic tree house.*

"Ahhh!" said Ben, settling into his chair. "Not much cooler here, though, is it?"

"No, but it's nice," said Annie.

"So, you wish to learn more about me?" said Ben. "Ask me anything!"

"Well, um . . . let's start with when you were a kid," said Annie.

Ben laughed. "Excellent starting place—when I was a baby goat!" he said. "My father made candles and soap, and I was one of fifteen children. We were so poor, I had only two years of school, then I had to go to work."

"Whoa. What did you do?" said Jack.

"I worked in my brother's printing office. At seventeen I left Boston and came to Philadelphia all by myself. I started my own printing shop. Soon I published a newspaper called the *Pennsylvania Gazette.* Then I created the first public library in North America, the one you just saw. I wrote and printed a bestselling yearly pamphlet called *Poor Richard's Almanack.*

"I started the first fire company in Philadelphia and the first post office. I invented the Franklin woodstove. I introduced cobblestones and street lamps to the city. I founded a college and a hospital. I grabbed electricity from the clouds in my famous kite experiment. And that led to my invention of the lightning rod.

"I supplied the army in the French and Indian War. I was elected to the Assembly of Pennsylvania. I was elected the first postmaster general of all the colonies. I helped write the Declaration of Independence.

"I was the American representative to England, France, and Sweden. I negotiated a treaty with England. And I became governor of Pennsylvania." Ben stopped to catch his breath.

"Is that *all*?" said Annie.

The three of them laughed.

"I knew I liked you," said Ben. "But since you asked, there *are* a few more things I've done. For instance, I invented bifocals. By the way, you have very nice glasses, Jack."

"Thanks," said Jack.

"And I invented a new kind of ship's anchor," said Ben. "I created a candle that makes a bright white light and lasts longer than other candles. I've written about waterspouts at sea and the origin of northern storms. I've kept journals about dolphins, crabs, and the moon."

"Wow," said Annie.

There was silence for a moment.

"Oh, I almost forgot," said Ben. "I've also studied ants and pigeons."

They all laughed again.

Then Ben sighed. "I'm afraid I must stop there because I am growing quite tired of talking about myself."

"Well, what are you doing *these* days?" Jack asked nervously. He knew Ben didn't want to talk about the meetings at the state house.

But, to Jack's surprise, Ben leaned forward in his chair. "Can you keep a secret?" he whispered.

"Yes!" Jack and Annie whispered back. They leaned closer to him.

"I tell you this in absolute secrecy," said Ben. "At the age of eighty-one, I am a delegate to the Constitutional Convention, working to help frame a Constitution for the United States."

"No!" whispered Annie.

"Yes!" whispered Ben. He sat back in his chair and grinned at them.

"So, when will the new Constitution be ready?" said Jack.

"That I do not know," said Ben. He sighed. He frowned. "In truth, dear Jack and Annie, I don't know if it will ever be ready."

"Why? What do you mean?" said Jack.

"The delegates disagree on so many things!" said Ben. "I worry about the stormy debates we have." He took off his glasses and rubbed his eyes. "Honestly, right now, I myself do not plan to sign the document."

"You don't?" said Annie.

"You don't?" said Jack.

Ben sighed again. He put his glasses back on and looked at them.

"No, children," he said. "I fear I do not."

7

Now's the Time

Jack took a deep breath. Now he fully understood their mission: they must get Doctor Benjamin Franklin to sign the Constitution of the United States.

Morgan had written:

In Old Philadelphia,
A paper must be signed.
Help Doctor Ben
Make up his mind.

Jack looked at Annie to see if she understood. She nodded.

"What is everyone arguing about?" Annie asked Ben.

"Some want a strong central government," said Ben, "and others do not. Some are not even sure democracy can work. Can we trust our citizens to rule themselves? Do we need a king? Will the small states have the same power as the big states? My greatest concern, though, is slavery. We *must* end it! But I fear that will not happen now."

"Oh, that's terrible," said Annie.

"Indeed, it is. On the other hand, there is a great need for a central government," said Ben. "We have no way to collect taxes. We have no way to select leaders." Ben took a deep breath. "I have almost lost hope, my friends. I fear we will never be one nation."

"Really?" said Jack. "Never?"

Ben shook his head. "I just do not see how we

can come to a fair agreement." He sighed, then yawned. He closed his eyes. In the next moment, his head fell to the side, and he started to snore.

"Oh, man, this is serious," Jack whispered to Annie. "If he doesn't sign the Constitution, I'll bet others won't, either. And without the Constitution, our country will never come together."

"Let's look at Morgan's note," said Annie.

Jack reached into his backpack and pulled out their rhyme. He read the last two stanzas:

Listen to his thoughts.
If his fears start to grow
And he loses all hope,
There's a place he must go.

'Tis a land filled with things
You see every day.
But these everyday wonders
Will show him the way.

"There's a place he must go," repeated Annie. "Read the last part again."

Jack reread the last four lines:

'Tis a land filled with things
You see every day.
But these everyday wonders
Will show him the way.

"I get it," said Annie. "Morgan's telling us to take Ben to Frog Creek. To *our* time."

"What?" said Jack. "No!"

"Yes!" said Annie. "She says go to a land with things we see every day. That's not America in 1787. That's America in our time."

"But we've never taken anyone home with us," said Jack. "Never!"

"I know. This will be so cool," said Annie. "We just have to get him up to the tree house."

She and Jack looked up. "Impossible," Jack said. "He can't climb the rope ladder."

"We have to try," said Annie. She tapped Ben's shoulder. "Excuse me?" she said. "Doctor . . . ?"

Ben stirred from his nap. "Yes?" he said. "Sorry, I must have dozed off."

"That's okay," said Annie. "Jack and I have a secret to tell you. A really big secret."

"Yes?" Ben sat up in his chair. He yawned and shook his head. "Tell me. What is it? I like secrets very much."

"There's a tree house in this tree," said Annie.

"In this very tree?" said Ben.

"Yes," said Annie. "But the big news is that it's magic. It can take you to the past—or to the future."

"Goodness. Yes, of course it can," said Ben. He winked at them. "I play games like this with my grandchildren."

"Um . . . this isn't a game," said Jack. "It's real."

"Real, indeed," said Ben, nodding. His eyes twinkled.

"No, seriously. It's real," said Annie, standing. "You can see a little of the tree house through the branches. Look up."

Ben leaned forward in his chair and looked up. "Oh . . . yes!" he said. "Goodness, I had no idea. Did Louis build that?"

"Um . . . no," said Jack.

Annie pulled the rope ladder out from its hiding place. "So, this is what we have to do," she said. "To get to the tree house, we have to climb this ladder."

"Oh, my, do you know how old I am, child?" asked Ben.

"You said you were eighty-one," said Annie. "But no one is too old for a little bit of magic."

"No, indeed!" said Ben, smiling. "I'm definitely

not too old for magic. Let's give it a try!" He stood up and grabbed the rope ladder.

"Go slowly, and we'll hold it steady," said Jack.

He and Annie held both sides of the ladder. Ben carefully climbed up through the mulberry tree and into the magic tree house.

"Oh, my!" Ben called from above.

Annie hurried after him. Jack grabbed Ben's walking stick and carried it up the ladder.

Inside the tree house, Ben looked amazed. "I had no idea this was here," he said. "How could I have missed it?"

"You missed it because it wasn't here until this morning," said Jack.

Annie picked up the Pennsylvania book. She found the picture of Frog Creek.

"Ready to see the future?" she asked.

Ben laughed. "Of course! I have always wanted to peek into the future."

"How about 2019?" said Annie.

"Why not? That sounds delightful!" said Ben. "You children have wondrous imaginations."

He still thinks we're playing a game, thought Jack. *We should probably do a better job of preparing him.*

"Okay. Now's the time!" said Annie.

"Wait—wait," said Jack. He was starting to worry that traveling through time might give Ben a heart attack.

Annie paid no attention. "I wish we could go there!" she exclaimed.

The wind started to blow.

The tree house started to spin.

It spun faster and faster.

Then everything was still.

Absolutely still.

8

Run for Your Lives!

It was still hot and muggy in the Frog Creek woods.

Jack and Annie were wearing their own clothes again. Ben's clothes hadn't changed. He had on the same outfit he'd worn in Old Philadelphia—from his white ruffled collar to his buckle shoes.

"What . . . what happened?" he asked Jack and Annie. He looked a bit dazed. "Where are we? What are you wearing?"

"These are the clothes we wear in *our* time, in 2019," said Annie. "The tree house brought you to our time and our hometown—Frog Creek, Pennsylvania."

"I—I don't understand," said Ben. He seemed to have difficulty breathing.

"Try to relax," Annie said softly. "I promise you're safe."

Ben closed his eyes. His breathing slowly returned to normal. "All right, I feel better now," he said.

Ben reached out the window and plucked a leaf from a branch of the oak tree. "Well, *this* is real," he said. "But it is all very strange. I wonder what science would have to say about this."

"I think we have to forget about science for now," said Jack. "Think of your journey to the future as a—"

"A big mystery," said Annie.

"A big mystery," Ben whispered. "Yes. There are many things science cannot explain. Time itself is a mystery."

"Exactly," said Jack. "Time is a mystery."

Ben shook his head. He looked troubled. Then he clapped his hands. "So be it! Time is a mystery!" He grinned. "Show me my future country!"

"Okay!" said Jack, relieved. "We'll go first and hold the ladder for you again."

Jack and Annie hurried down the rope ladder. Annie carried Ben's walking stick under her arm. Then she and Jack held the ladder steady for Ben.

Ben climbed down slowly. When he reached the ground, he looked around with amazement.

"Ready to take a walk?" said Annie.

"Yes, yes!" said Ben. "Lead the way!"

Annie handed Ben his walking stick. Then they all started through the woods. As they walked, Ben smiled at the trees and birds. "Maple, oak, beech, robin, wren, woodpecker," he said. "No different from the ones at home . . ."

Jack stopped at the edge of the woods. "Okay.

Some things outside the woods *will* be different," he said to Ben. "I just want to warn you."

"Don't be afraid," said Annie.

"Oh, my dear, I have been all over the world," Ben said. "I have lived in France and England. I have spent time with kings and queens. I even helped fight a revolution. I fear nothing."

"Great. Let's go," said Jack. He and Annie led Ben out of the woods.

"What is *that*?" said Ben, startled. He pointed his walking stick at the road. "Your roadway—it is smooth and black!"

"It's paved with asphalt," said Jack.

Ben stooped to feel the road. "Oh, my . . . so flat and clean!" he said.

"Yeah, I guess," said Jack. He'd never thought much about a smoothly paved road. But at this moment, it *did* seem special, compared to the dirty, bumpy cobblestone streets in Ben's city.

A green station wagon came around the corner. The driver honked her horn.

"Ahhh!" Ben said, jumping back. He stared after the car as it drove down the road. "What—what was *that*?"

"A car," said Annie.

"Cars are like carts and buggies," Jack said quickly, "except they have engines instead of horses. They move much faster."

"They won't hurt you," said Annie, "if you don't step into the street in front of them."

Ben pulled out his handkerchief. "Oh my goodness. All right . . . ," he murmured, wiping his face. "That was *truly* amazing."

"It's pretty ordinary to us," said Annie.

"Really?" said Ben. "Then let us proceed."

They started up the sidewalk. Jack was relieved that Frog Creek was an old-fashioned-looking town. Most houses were not that different from the ones in Ben's time.

But Ben pointed to a sprinkler spraying a lawn. “What is that?” he said.

“It waters the grass,” said Jack.

“Ah,” said Ben. He pointed at the power lines

alongside the road. "I don't understand—why are your clotheslines so high?"

Annie laughed. "Those aren't clotheslines! They're power lines and telephone lines," she said.

"The power lines carry electricity into all the buildings," said Jack. "And—"

"*My* electricity?" said Ben.

"Uh . . . not really," said Jack. "We don't get our electricity from lightning. It comes from burning coal and gas and oil in these big machines . . . that . . . um . . ."

"Make electricity," Annie finished.

"I'm still not sure I understand," said Ben.

Annie leaned closer to Ben. "We don't, either," she whispered.

Ben stopped. "What is that strange noise?" he said. "That loud buzzing? Is it coming from overhead?"

They all looked up. The buzzing grew into a

roar. A small propeller plane appeared above the treetops. It had taken off from the nearby airfield.

"AHHH!" Ben cried. "Run for your lives!" Then he covered his head and hobbled quickly back into the Frog Creek woods.

9

A Good Idea

"Ben, wait for us!" yelled Annie.

Jack and Annie hurried into the woods after Ben Franklin. They found him huddled beneath a tree.

"That was an airplane," said Jack. "It won't hurt you. And it won't fall out of the sky."

"But why not?" said Ben.

Jack only half remembered how planes flew. "Well, it has an engine that pushes it forward," he said. "Then air under the wings helps lift it up."

"It all works together. Somehow," said Annie.

"Oh, my," said Ben. "Does your world have many airplanes?"

"Thousands," said Annie. "Huge ones called jets."

"And rockets," said Jack. "Some rockets can go all the way to the moon."

"Impossible!" said Ben.

"I can see why that might seem impossible, but these are everyday things to us," said Annie.

"We don't even think about them," said Jack.

"Your world does not seem real to me!" said Ben. "The trees and grass and squirrels are real, but not lines that carry electricity and rockets that go to the moon!" He wiped his face with his handkerchief. "I fear there is no place for me here. I am a plain and simple man."

"No, you're not! You're a genius!" said Annie.

"Not here, my dear," Ben said. "My little

inventions and experiments are nothing compared to carriages that roar and machines that fly. I believe it is time for me to go home."

"Wait—uh—have you made a decision about what you're going to do?" said Jack. "I mean about signing the Constitution?"

"No. But it doesn't matter if I sign or not," said Ben. "We delegates think our ideas are so very important. But now I see they matter little in your world."

"That's not true at all!" said Annie. "They matter a lot."

Ben smiled sadly. "Children, please. Lead me to the tree house," he said.

"But—" said Annie.

"Please," said Ben. "I want to go home."

Jack looked at Annie. She nodded. "Okay," said Jack.

"Follow us," Annie said gently.

She and Jack started leading Ben back through the Frog Creek woods.

"Morgan was wrong," Annie whispered to Jack. "She said our everyday wonders would show Ben the way."

"I know. They only confuse him," said Jack. He felt terrible. Not only had they failed to change Ben's mind about signing the Constitution, they'd also upset one of the world's greatest heroes.

By the time they reached the tree house, Ben looked pale and weary. "I apologize for being such a bad guest," he said.

"*You* don't have to apologize," said Jack. "*We* apologize."

"No, no. You have only been kind," said Ben.

"Wait, Ben!" said Annie. "Before you go, there's something you really, really have to see."

"What?" Jack whispered to her.

"Trust me!" Annie whispered. Then she turned to Ben. "I promise you'll like this—it's really great!"

Ben sighed. "All right. Lead me there," he said.

"This way," said Annie.

Jack and Annie followed Ben through the woods to the sidewalk. As they headed up the street, the air felt hotter and more humid than ever.

"Is this place far away?" Ben asked.

"No, it's just ahead," said Annie. "See that building?"

She pointed to a brick building with tall paned windows.

"Oh, man," whispered Jack. "Brilliant."

Annie was taking Ben to the Frog Creek Library!

"Don't worry if people stare at you," Annie said to Ben. "We'll tell them you're in rehearsals for a play and you're still wearing your costume."

Ben looked puzzled, but he nodded and followed Annie and Jack up the library steps. Jack opened the front door, and they all stepped inside.

Ben took a deep breath. "Ah, the cool air in this room is delightful," he said. "Another invention?"

"It *is*," said Jack. He usually didn't think much about air-conditioning, but today it was definitely delightful.

"And what a wonderful room!" said Ben.

The library walls were lined with bookshelves. People of all ages and colors sat in armchairs, reading books, magazines, and newspapers. Some were working at computers.

"See what you started in Philadelphia?" Annie said. "Now we have free public libraries all over America. Thousands of them. They make a difference to all kinds of people."

The librarian looked up from her desk. "Jack and Annie!" she said. "Hi!"

"Hi, Sandy!" they said.

"You've brought Ben Franklin!" Sandy said, grinning. "What's going on?"

"We're in rehearsals for a play," said Jack.

"We need to look some things up," said Annie, "to help our friend play his part."

"Please. Go ahead," said the librarian.

"What play?" Ben whispered.

"We'll show you," said Annie. She led Ben to a bulletin board announcing community events.

Jack pointed to a small theater poster. "See? *Ben Franklin in Paris,*" he said. "You're famous in history. Actors have played you in musicals, movies, and TV shows."

"Movies? TV?" said Ben.

"It's hard to explain," said Annie.

"Your face is on our hundred-dollar bill," said Jack.

"No!" said Ben.

"Yes!" said Jack and Annie together.

"My goodness," said Ben. "That's wonderful."

Ben studied the other notices on the bulletin board. They announced church meetings, yard sales, bake sales, a fire station picnic, a Fourth of July parade. . . .

"OPEN TO ALL," Ben read at the top of the bulletin board. Then he looked around at the library. "This place is open to all, too, isn't it?" he said. "You have a wonderful community here, I can tell."

"There are lots of libraries and communities like this everywhere," said Annie.

"And so many children are reading," said Ben. "Where did they all learn to read?"

"America has free schools for everyone," said Annie. "No matter how poor you are or where you come from. And girls get the same education as boys."

"At least twelve years for everyone," said Jack.

Ben's eyes grew teary. "I would have liked

that," he said softly. "There was so much I wanted to learn."

"Well, wait till you see *this*," said Annie. She led Ben to a table. "Please sit down."

"What is this machine?" said Ben.

"It's called a computer," said Jack.

10

WE THE PEOPLE

"A computer?" said Ben. He stared at the large desktop machine.

"Yes, that's right," said Annie. "It's useful for learning all about the world. Lots of people even carry small computers in their pockets. On smart phones."

"Phones?" said Ben. "What are *phones*?"

"Uh, hard to explain. Let's look at this computer now," said Jack.

Annie and Jack grabbed chairs and sat next to Ben.

"Watch," said Jack. He tapped a key, and the screen lit up.

Ben gasped.

"Wait," said Jack. He did a search for "United States of America." Then he clicked on an entry.

A map of the United States and the country's Great Seal appeared on the screen.

"Oh! How did that happen? Where did that come from?" Ben asked.

"That's hard to explain, too," said Annie. "But read what it says."

Ben read aloud softly from the screen:

The United States is a country of fifty states. Stretching from the Atlantic to the Pacific Oceans, it covers a vast part of North America. It has a population of more than 325 million people. Since its founding, immigrants from all over the globe have moved to the United States and become citizens.

"My goodness!" whispered Ben.

Jack pointed to the Great Seal of the United States at the top of the screen. "That's a symbol for our country," he said.

"I know that symbol," said Ben. "In 1776, I was on a committee to create it." He read the writing on the seal. "'*E pluribus unum.*' That's Latin for 'Out of many, one.'"

"Right, out of many, one," said Annie. "Our teacher told us what that means: The United States is made up of many different states, and people from all over the world. But we are all *one* nation."

"Yes! Yes!" said Ben. "I wonder if our delegates have forgotten those words."

"Probably," said Annie. "People forget them in our time, too."

"It's so important to come together as one country," said Ben. "But how can we do that? We are very divided."

"Maybe the different sides have to keep talking to each other, and listening to each other, and agree to go forward." said Annie.

"She's right," said Jack. "Don't forget—you can add important stuff later. They'll be called amendments. Like amendments that guarantee freedom of speech and freedom of religion."

"And give women the vote!" said Annie.

"And end slavery and give *everyone* equal rights," said Jack.

"Yes, yes . . . that makes sense," Ben said.

"Perhaps creating a Constitution is only the *first* step . . . not the last."

"Exactly!" said Jack.

Ben stood up. "I must go now. I must go home. I have to be back for the afternoon session. This Constitution is *very* important! They need me to be there. *You* need me to be there!"

"We do!" said Annie.

Ben hobbled across the library, heading for the door.

"Good-bye, Ben!" Sandy the librarian called. "Have a good show!"

Readers looked up from their books and stared as Ben Franklin hurried outside.

Jack and Annie caught up with Ben in front of the library. The three of them walked quickly to the sidewalk.

"My world may seem very rough and simple compared with yours," Ben said breathlessly.

"But 'tis filled with the discovery of new things and new ideas! Why, I can even help create a Constitution that will change the history of the world!"

"You can!" said Annie.

"Of course, there are parts that I absolutely do not agree with," said Ben. "But additions, as you said, and changes—*amendments*—will be made later. First, we must come together to create *one country*. We may never get another chance."

"That's true," said Jack.

"This way!" said Annie. She and Jack led Ben into the woods. In spite of the heat, Ben moved quickly between the trees.

"Here we are!" Jack said when they reached the oak tree.

Jack and Annie held the ladder steady. Ben tucked his walking stick under his arm and climbed up slowly.

Once Ben was inside the tree house, Jack grabbed the ladder to follow him. But then he heard Ben say, "Hello, my good lady . . . !"

The sound of a woman's voice came from the tree house.

Jack froze at the bottom of the ladder.

"Jack! It's *her*!" said Annie.

"I know!" Jack said. They looked up.

"Morgan!" cried Annie.

Morgan le Fay and Ben Franklin stood at the tree house window together.

"Hello, Jack! Hello, Annie!" Morgan called. "Congratulations! You successfully carried out my wishes on your last four adventures. You learned a great lesson from Jackie Robinson. You worked with Mother Mary Joseph in Texas. You spent time with Emperor Marcus Aurelius of Rome."

"And you have just given *me* one of the most remarkable adventures of my life!" said Ben. "You have showed me the wonders of your world. All people here—men, women, black, white, young, old—are to be treated equally. This country is full of different communities and different people. And yet it is one country."

"Yes!" said Jack.

"Please, Jack and Annie, never take all the wondrous things of your world for granted," said Ben. "Promise me you will always be filled with curiosity and wonder."

"We promise!" said Jack and Annie.

"Thank you again for everything!" said Ben.

"Farewell!" called Morgan.

A mighty swirl of wind—

a flash of lightning—

a crack of thunder—

and the magic tree house, Morgan le Fay, and Benjamin Franklin were gone!

Jack and Annie stared up at the top of the oak for a long moment. Then they both sighed and started walking through the woods.

"Remember in Morgan's rhyme, Morgan says, 'Everyday wonders will show Ben the way,'" said Annie. "At first, I thought she meant modern inventions."

"Me too," said Jack. "But those things just seemed to scare Ben."

"Right," said Annie. "So then I thought, what if we show him the public library? He wouldn't be afraid of that."

"Yeah, especially since he started the first one," said Jack. "And he'd get to see how everyone's allowed to go there and borrow books and use computers—"

"And get tons of information," said Annie. "Like how cars work."

"And planes," said Jack, "and electricity."

Annie stopped walking. "So let's go back," she said.

"Where?"

"There."

"Now?"

"Now."

"Why not?"

Without another word, Jack and Annie started running through the summer heat, heading back to the Frog Creek Library.

FROG CREEK LIBRARY

MORE FACTS FOR YOU AND JACK

On September 17, 1787, the Constitution of the United States was signed. Benjamin Franklin felt that the document was not perfect, but he urged everyone to be humble and stand together in the spirit of compromise.

By 1791, ten amendments, known as the Bill of Rights, were added to the Constitution.

Since that time, more amendments have been added. Today the Constitution includes twenty-seven amendments.

The United States Constitution is the supreme law of the nation. It is the longest-standing constitution in the history of the world.

The Latin phrase *E pluribus unum,* meaning "Out of many, one," appears on every U.S. coin.

Turn the page for a sneak peek at

Magic Tree House® Fact Tracker

Benjamin Franklin

1

Benjamin Franklin

Benjamin Franklin was born more than three hundred years ago. Today he is still one of the most famous and beloved men in American history. Benjamin was a great scientist, thinker, inventor, writer, and printer. He created or helped create the first lending library, the first fire department, the first public hospital, and the first post office in America.

When he wasn't working, Benjamin used his spare time wisely. He played music and taught himself five languages. He also learned to swim, and many years after he died, he was made a member of the International Swimming Hall of Fame!

Although people today think of him as <u>Ben</u>, he did not use that nickname.

But Benjamin is probably best known as one of America's Founding Fathers. His wisdom helped guide the country in

its struggle to break free from English rule and become a new nation.

People often wonder how this poor boy, with just two years of school, was able to lead such an amazing life. Benjamin Franklin's story is hard to believe.

Boston

Benjamin was born in Boston, Massachusetts, in 1706. At the time of his birth, the United States wasn't a country. It was divided into thirteen colonies and ruled by England, a country thousands of miles across the ocean.

Boston was part of the Massachusetts Bay Colony. Because the city is on the Atlantic Ocean and has a deep harbor, it was one of the busiest seaports in the colonies.

At the printshop Benjamin often read articles in a journal called the *Spectator.* He tried to write the same articles from memory. After he finished writing, he'd read the *Spectator* again. If he didn't think what he'd written was good enough, he'd rewrite it over and over.

Benjamin became an excellent writer. Throughout his life he produced books and thousands of letters and articles. He sent or received over 15,000 letters in his life! His most famous book is the story of his life.

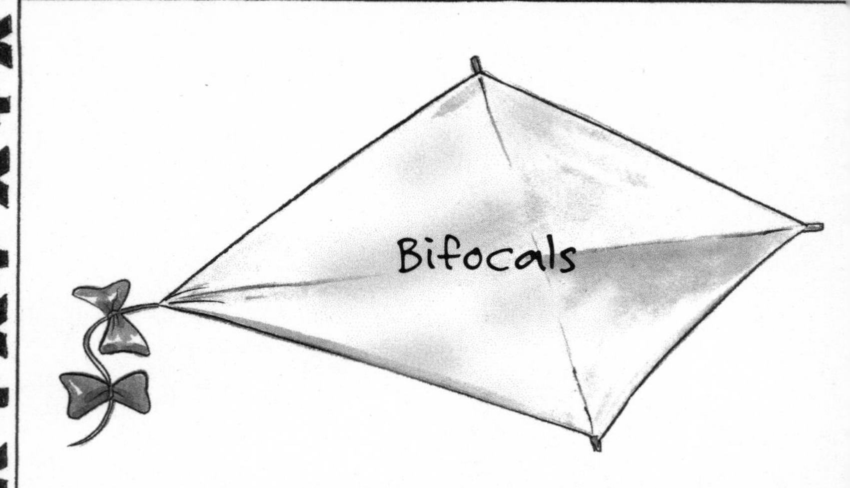

Benjamin needed one pair of glasses to see things up close and a second pair to see far away. He carried around two pairs of glasses to deal with this.

Trying to remember to bring two pairs of glasses was so annoying that in 1779, Benjamin decided to do something about it. He came up with a great idea. Why not put two different lenses together in one pair of glasses?

He had lenses in each set of glasses

cut in half. Then he had an optician join the two halves together into one frame. The top lens was for seeing far away, and the lower one was for reading close up. Benjamin had solved his problem! He called the new glasses double spectacles, but today we call them bifocals.

If you see glasses with a faint line running through the middle of the lenses, you're looking at bifocals!

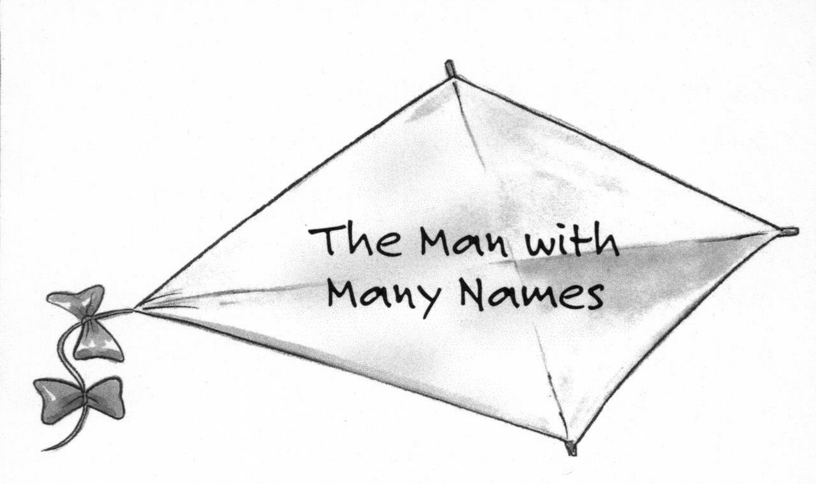

The Man with Many Names

Benjamin Franklin has many nicknames. Because of all the work he did for the colonies and the United States, he is sometimes called the First American. This nickname was given to him after he died.

However, some nicknames were given to him during his life. When he was in England, most of the workers at the printer's drank beer. Benjamin always drank water, so people called him Water-American.

Some names Benjamin gave himself. Writers in Benjamin's days often used fake names to sign their work. Benjamin used many different names! Silence Dogood is probably his most famous, but here are some others:

Magic Tree House®

#1: Dinosaurs Before Dark
#2: The Knight at Dawn
#3: Mummies in the Morning
#4: Pirates Past Noon
#5: Night of the Ninjas
#6: Afternoon on the Amazon
#7: Sunset of the Sabertooth
#8: Midnight on the Moon
#9: Dolphins at Daybreak
#10: Ghost Town at Sundown
#11: Lions at Lunchtime
#12: Polar Bears Past Bedtime
#13: Vacation Under the Volcano
#14: Day of the Dragon King
#15: Viking Ships at Sunrise
#16: Hour of the Olympics
#17: Tonight on the *Titanic*
#18: Buffalo Before Breakfast
#19: Tigers at Twilight
#20: Dingoes at Dinnertime
#21: Civil War on Sunday
#22: Revolutionary War on Wednesday
#23: Twister on Tuesday
#24: Earthquake in the Early Morning
#25: Stage Fright on a Summer Night
#26: Good Morning, Gorillas
#27: Thanksgiving on Thursday
#28: High Tide in Hawaii
#29: A Big Day for Baseball
#30: Hurricane Heroes in Texas
#31: Warriors in Winter

Magic Tree House® Merlin Missions

#1: Christmas in Camelot
#2: Haunted Castle on Hallows Eve
#3: Summer of the Sea Serpent
#4: Winter of the Ice Wizard
#5: Carnival at Candlelight
#6: Season of the Sandstorms
#7: Night of the New Magicians
#8: Blizzard of the Blue Moon
#9: Dragon of the Red Dawn
#10: Monday with a Mad Genius
#11: Dark Day in the Deep Sea
#12: Eve of the Emperor Penguin
#13: Moonlight on the Magic Flute
#14: A Good Night for Ghosts
#15: Leprechaun in Late Winter
#16: A Ghost Tale for Christmas Time
#17: A Crazy Day with Cobras
#18: Dogs in the Dead of Night
#19: Abe Lincoln at Last!
#20: A Perfect Time for Pandas
#21: Stallion by Starlight
#22: Hurry Up, Houdini!
#23: High Time for Heroes
#24: Soccer on Sunday
#25: Shadow of the Shark
#26: Balto of the Blue Dawn
#27: Night of the Ninth Dragon

Magic Tree House®
Super Editions

#1: World at War, 1944

Magic Tree House®
Fact Trackers

Dinosaurs
Knights and Castles
Mummies and Pyramids
Pirates
Rain Forests
Space
Titanic
Twisters and Other Terrible Storms
Dolphins and Sharks
Ancient Greece and the Olympics
American Revolution
Sabertooths and the Ice Age
Pilgrims
Ancient Rome and Pompeii
Tsunamis and Other Natural Disasters
Polar Bears and the Arctic
Sea Monsters
Penguins and Antarctica
Leonardo da Vinci
Ghosts
Leprechauns and Irish Folklore
Rags and Riches: Kids in the Time of Charles Dickens
Snakes and Other Reptiles
Dog Heroes
Abraham Lincoln
Pandas and Other Endangered Species
Horse Heroes
Heroes for All Times
Soccer
Ninjas and Samurai
China: Land of the Emperor's Great Wall
Sharks and Other Predators
Vikings
Dogsledding and Extreme Sports
Dragons and Mythical Creatures
World War II
Baseball
Wild West
Texas
Warriors
Benjamin Franklin

More Magic Tree House®

Games and Puzzles from the Tree House
Magic Tricks from the Tree House
My Magic Tree House Journal
Magic Tree House Survival Guide
Animals Games and Puzzles
Magic Tree House Incredible Fact Book